Smartypantus Rulus O.K.us

First Sandcastle Books edition published in 1991
by G. P. Putnam's Sons, a division of
The Putnam & Grosset Group,
200 Madison Avenue, New York, NY 10016.
Sandcastle Books and the Sandcastle logo
are trademarks belonging to
The Putnam & Grosset Group.
First published by Hamish Hamilton Children's Books.
Printed in Hong Kong

Library of Congress Cataloging-in-Publication Data
Cole, Babette. Princess Smartypants.
Summary: Not wishing to marry any of her royal suitors, Princess
Smartypants devises difficult tasks at which they all fail,
until the multitalented Prince Swashbuckle appears.
[1. Fairy tales] I. Title.
PZ8.C667Pr 1987 [E] 86-12381
ISBN 0-399-21409-7 (hardcover)
7 9 10 8 6
ISBN 0-399-21779-7 (Sandcastle)
5 7 9 10 8 6

Princess SmartyPants
by
Babette Cole

G. P. Putnam's Sons · New York

Princess Smartypants did not want to get married. She enjoyed being a Ms.

Because she was very pretty and rich, all
the princes wanted her to be their Mrs.

Princess Smartypants wanted to live in her castle

with her pets and do exactly as she pleased.

"It's high time you smartened yourself up," said her Mother, the Queen. "Stop messing about with those animals and find yourself a husband!"

Suitors were always turning up at the
castle making a nuisance of themselves.
    "Right," declared Princess Smartypants,
"whoever can accomplish the tasks that
I set will, as they say, win my hand."

She asked Prince Compost to stop the slugs from eating her garden.

She asked Prince Rushforth
to feed her pets.

She challenged
Prince Pelvis to a roller-disco marathon.

She invited Prince Boneshaker for a
cross-country ride on her motorbike.

She called on Prince Vertigo
to rescue her from her tower.

She sent Prince Bashthumb to chop

some firewood in the royal forest.

She suggested to Prince Fetlock that he
might like to put her pony through its paces.

She told Prince Grovel to take her Mother, the Queen, shopping.

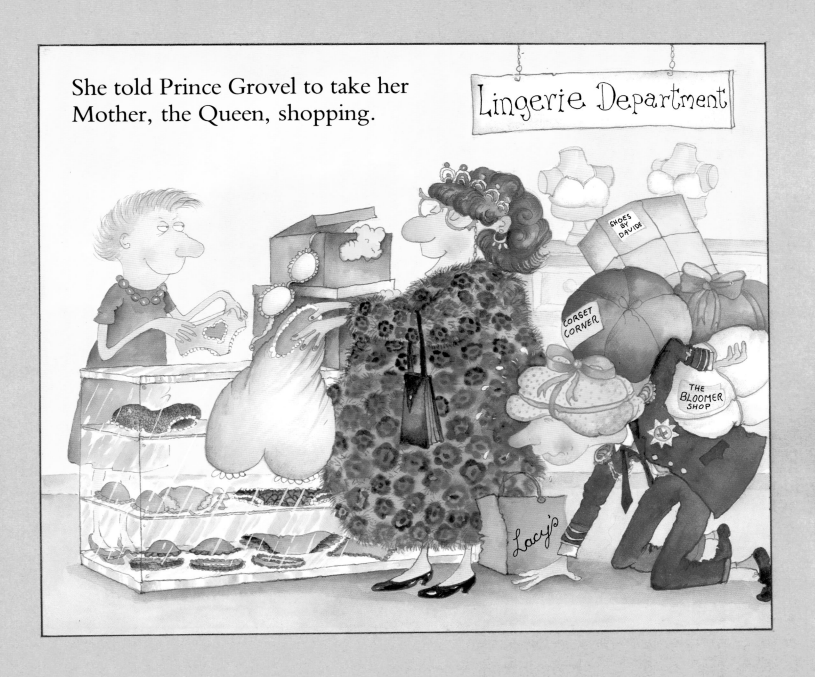

She commanded Prince Swimbladder to retrieve her magic ring from the goldfish pond.

None of the princes could accomplish the task he was set. They all left in disgrace.

"That's that, then," said Smartypants, thinking she was safe.

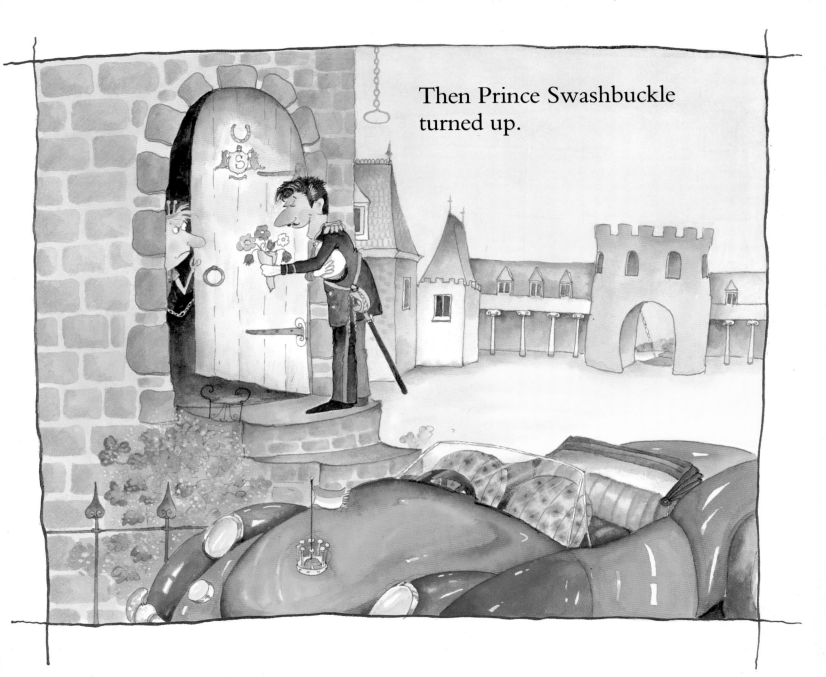

Then Prince Swashbuckle
turned up.

He stopped the slugs eating her garden . . .

. . . fed her pets . . .

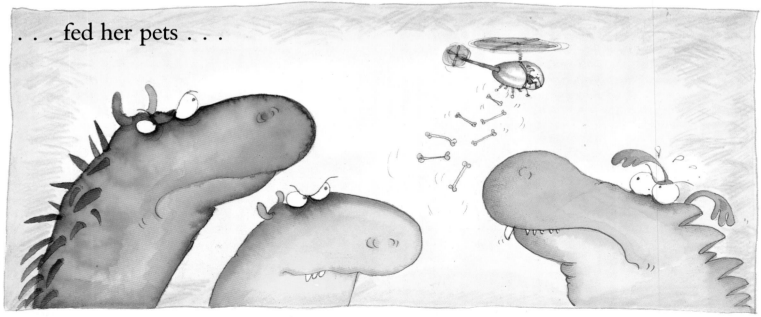

. . . roller-discoed
until dawn . . .

. . . rode for miles on
her motorbike . . .

He rescued her
from her tower.

He found some firewood in the forest.

He even tamed her horrid pony . . .

. . . took her Mother, the Queen, shopping

and retrieved her magic ring from the goldfish pond.

Prince Swashbuckle didn't think Princess Smartypants was so smart.

So she gave him a magic kiss . . .

. . . and he turned into a
gigantic warty toad!

Prince Swashbuckle left in a big hurry!

When the other princes heard
what had happened to Prince
Swashbuckle, none of them
wanted to marry Smartypants . . .

. . . so she lived
happily ever after.